GLORIA MAYA

The Good And The Bad Witch.

AuthorHouse™
1663 Liberty Drive
Bloomington, IN 47403
www.authorhouse.com
Phone: 833-262-8899

Because of the dynamic nature of the Internet, any web addresses or links contained in this book may have changed since publication and may no longer be valid. The views expressed in this work are solely those of the author and do not necessarily reflect the views of the publisher, and the publisher hereby disclaims any responsibility for them.

Any people depicted in stock imagery provided by Getty Images are models, and such images are being used for illustrative purposes only. Certain stock imagery © Getty Images.

This book is printed on acid-free paper.

ISBN: 978-1-6655-1233-6 (sc)
978-1-6655-1234-3 (e)

Print information available on the last page.

Published by AuthorHouse 09/07/2021

authorHOUSE®

The Good And The Bad Witch.

"A Fairy Tale
of two little witches

This book belongs to:

_____

This book is dedicated to
My LITTLEST Guardian
ANGEL GABRIEL 02/19/82 -
06/20/84, his brothers and
to all the children.

"*A* long long time ago there lived a beautiful little good witch and an old old ugly little bad witch both of these two little witches lived in the forest .

Their names were Briella and Abigail. Briella's Castle looked almost like Cinderella's except Briella had a favorite color and it was pink. Everything she had and wore was pink.

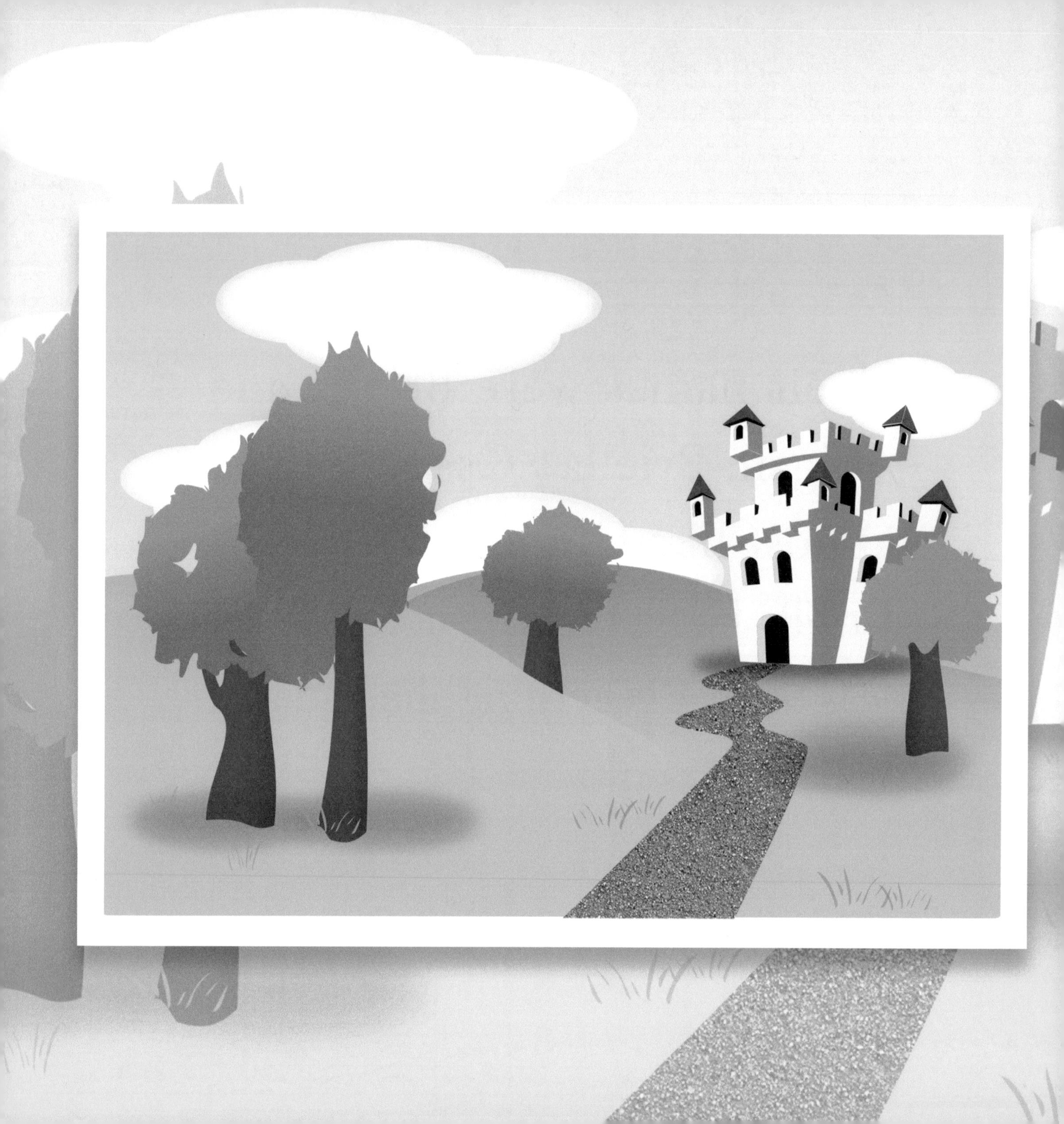

These two little witches lived in very big castles in the middle of a field of beautiful wild life. There were flowers, trees, bunny rabbits, squirrels, and colorful pretty birds.

The animals were kind and gentle. Children loved to hang out in this beautiful forest of wild and gentle animals.

Abigail's castle's was not so pretty it was very spooky and scary. Her castle was dark and cold. There were crawling little creatures everywhere you looked. There were spiders, cobwebs ,and in the corner of her castle hanging from the ceiling there was a Giant beehive.

The honey Honey bees buzzed and fuzzed throughout her Castle. Briella and Abigail had two things in common they both loved to hop on their broom stick and go for an afternoon ride every day.

Every afternoon the beautiful pretty little witch Briella would jump on her sparkly bright pink broom stick. And up and away she fly to the sky Boom Boom Swish and swish she made loud swishing noises with her broom. Making dark and smokey circles up in the sky and the children below could see Briella and Abigail playing with their broomsticks trying to make loud sounds and shapes with their smokey broomsticks.

One day Abigail wanted to play tricks on the children that were watching them. She said I'm going to snatch them and lock them in my castle.

But Briella told Abigail I won't let you instead I will snatch them before you do. And take them to my beautiful sparkly Pink castle. And there they can play with all my toys till they get tired and then I will take them home one by one on my little witches' broom.

My name is

_____

What I learn in this book:

_____

_____

_____

_____

_____

_____

_____

_____

_____

LET'S KNOW ABOUT THE AUTHOR!

Gloria Maya is a loving mother to her 4 wonderful sons. She is a health worker and drives a school bus part time. Her youngest son, when he was five years old, inspired her to write this bed time story.

Printed in the United States
by Baker & Taylor Publisher Services